TULSA CITY-COUNTY LIBRARY

W9-AOM-927

Bulldogs

Leo Statts

abdopublishing.com

Published by Abdo Zoom™, PO Box 398166, Minneapolis, Minnesota 55439. Copyright © 2017 by Abdo Consulting Group, Inc. International copyrights reserved in all countries. No part of this book may be reproduced in any form without written permission from the publisher. Abdo Zoom™ is a trademark and logo of Abdo Consulting Group, Inc.

Printed in the United States of America, North Mankato, Minnesota
062016
092016

THIS BOOK CONTAINS
RECYCLED MATERIALS

Cover Photo: iStockphoto, cover
Interior Photos: iStockphoto, 1, 9; ChickenStock Images/Shutterstock Images, 5; WilleeCole Photography/Shutterstock Images, 6; Johnny Dao/Shutterstock Images, 8; Shutterstock Images, 10–11; Runa Kazakova/Shutterstock Images, 12; Nancy Paiva/iStockphoto, 13; Marina Masiennikova/iStock, 15; Pisaphotography/Shutterstock Images, 16; Trelawne Aimee/iStockphoto, 17; Jacob SjAman Svensson/iStockphoto, 18; Library of Congress, 19; Red Line Editorial, 20 (left), 20 (right), 21 (left), 21 (right)

Editor: Emily Temple
Series Designer: Madeline Berger
Art Direction: Dorothy Toth

Publisher's Cataloging-in-Publication Data
Names: Statts, Leo, author.
Title: Bulldogs / by Leo Statts.
Description: Minneapolis, MN : Abdo Zoom, [2017] | Series: Dogs | Includes
    bibliographical references and index.
Identifiers: LCCN 2016941129 | ISBN 9781680791723 (lib. bdg.) |
    ISBN 9781680793406 (ebook) | ISBN 9781680794298 (Read-to-me ebook)
Subjects: LCSH: Bulldogs (Dog breed)--Juvenile literature.
Classification: DDC 636.72--dc23
LC record available at http://lccn.loc.gov/2016941129

Table of Contents

Bulldogs

Bulldogs are short and strong.
They can look mean and grumpy.
But they are kind dogs.

Body

Bulldogs come in many colors. Their **coats** are short and shiny.

A bulldog has strong features. Its head is large.

It has big **wrinkles** on its face.
It has a **droopy** mouth.

Care

Bulldogs should be brushed once a week. They should be cleaned often.

A bulldog should go
on a walk each day.

Be careful of the weather.
Bulldogs get too hot
or too cold easily.

Personality

Bulldogs are calm dogs.
They like sleeping or sitting quietly.

They are loving and protective. They are great family dogs.

History

Bulldogs came from
the British Isles.

Today they can be
found all over the world.

17

Bulldogs are the fourth most popular dog breed.

US President Warren G. Harding had a bulldog.

19

Average Weight

A bulldog weighs the same as a full suitcase.

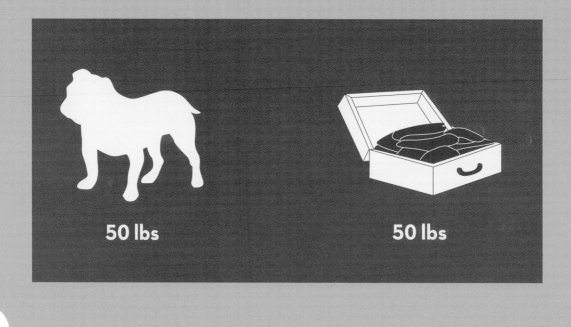

50 lbs

50 lbs

Average Height

A bulldog is taller than a basketball.

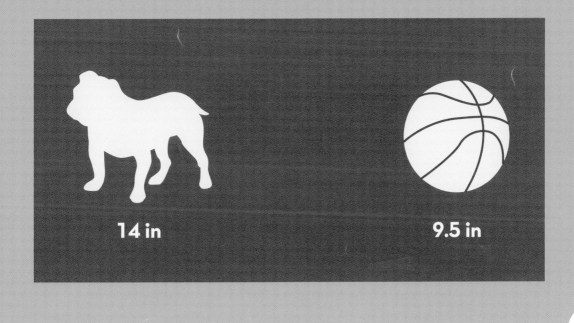

14 in

9.5 in

Glossary

breed – a group of animals sharing the same looks and features.

coat - the hair that covers an animal's body.

droopy - hanging down limply.

feature - a part of the face or body.

popular - liked by many people.

protective - to keep safe from harm.

wrinkle - a line or fold in the skin.

Booklinks

For more information
on **bulldogs**, please visit
booklinks.abdopublishing.com

Zoom In on Animals!

Learn even more with the Abdo Zoom
Animals database. Check out
abdozoom.com for more information.

Index